Dear reader,

I was diagnosed with dyslexia when I was halfway
through my English degree. I was twenty-one.
I'd been feeling frustrated that I kept getting
low marks even though I was working really hard.

The diagnosis explained my poor spelling and why I read so quickly (because
I don't read all the words). It also helped explain my awful sense of direction,
why I'm often a few minutes late and why I've always found it hard to
remember a long list of things unless I write them down.

I've always loved books, both reading them and writing my own stories. I knew
being dyslexic wouldn't stop me becoming an author because I've always seen
it as a strength. It helps me to look at things differently and make connections
that other people might not see. It helps me dream up ideas, worlds, and characters.

Just as Trixie discovers in this story, having dyslexia can sometimes be hard, but it
can also be pretty wonderful.

Thunderboots was my Grandpa's nickname for me when I was little and this story
means a lot to me. I hope you enjoy it.

Naomi X

For James, who has always believed in me. N.J.
For my daughter Tate—a proud dyslexic. R.A.

Great Clarendon Street, Oxford OX2 6DP

Oxford University Press is a department of the University of Oxford.
It furthers the University's objective of excellence in research, scholarship,
and education by publishing worldwide. Oxford is a registered trade mark
of Oxford University Press in the UK and in certain other countries

Text © Naomi Jones 2023

Illustrations © Rebecca Ashdown 2023

The moral rights of the author and artist have been asserted

Database right Oxford University Press (maker)

First published 2023

British Library Cataloguing in Publication Data available

ISBN: 978-0-19-277902-1

1 3 5 7 9 10 8 6 4 2

Text set in EDUK FS Me, developed as an inclusive typeface

Printed in China

Paper used in the production of this book is a natural, recyclable product made
from wood grown in sustainable forests. The manufacturing process conforms
to the environmental regulations of the country of origin

Naomi Jones   Rebecca Ashdown

THUNDER BOOTS

OXFORD
UNIVERSITY PRESS

Trixie was the smallest person in Primrose Tower.
She was also the loudest.

She loved to run and
jump up the stairs . . .

Thump!

'Wheee!'

cartwheel down
the corridors . . .

and dance into
her flat.

Everyone in Primrose Tower knew when Trixie was home.
They even had a special name for her—Thunderboots.

One day Trixie was big enough to start school.

She ran out of her flat and jumped down the stairs.

'Yippee!'

'Good luck, Thunderboots!'

'Enjoy school!'

'Have fun!'

Everyone was there to wish her good luck.

Trixie loved school.

She loved her teacher, Miss Fry, and her new friends.
She loved playing in the playground . . .

and eating lunch in the hall.

'Has anyone seen
my water bottle?'

She especially loved all the exciting things there were to learn.

Trixie learned numbers . . .

and the sounds letters made.

Learning how to write her
name was really fun!

Miss Fry read them a different story every day—
Trixie thought ones about dragons were the best.

'Whoosh!'

Sometimes she liked to imagine she was in her own dragon story!

'Trixie, are you listening?'

ROAR

Trixie's absolute favourite lesson was PE because she could run . . .

jump . . .

cartwheel . . .

and dance lots and lots and lots!

Miss Fry always asked them to warm up
first by doing some stretches.

'Stretch up high, then reach from side
to side before you touch your toes.'

It was a lot to remember.

'Whoops!'

Trixie tried to learn her letters . . .

and practise writing
every single day.

i lov
yoo
bAddy

But even after all that hard work, she still found it tricky.

Lily was the first person in the whole class to get a reading book. But when Lily showed it to Trixie she couldn't turn the letters into words.

The letters started to dance on the page instead.

'Sam has a cat.'

'Sma ahs a cat.'

Trixie was quiet for the rest of the day.

When she got back to Primrose Tower,
she tiptoed up the stairs so quietly
that nobody knew she was home.

'Is it the weekend soon?' Trixie asked Dad at bedtime.
Dad shook his head. 'It's Thursday today, so tomorrow is . . .'

'Tuesday?' guessed Trixie. But Dad
said Friday came next, *then*
it was the weekend.

In a quiet voice, Trixie said she wished it was the weekend tomorrow.
She said she didn't want to go to school any more.
Just as quietly, Dad asked why.

So Trixie told him. She told him that learning sounds
and letters was hard, that writing was hard,
and that remembering all the things
Miss Fry said was hard.

Trixie said everything felt hard.

S r p b u
w p b
h T F
x

Dad gave Trixie a big soft hug.

'Everyone learns differently and in different ways and that's OK.'

'It is?' Trixie asked.

Dad nodded. 'I'm just like you! I learn differently to other people too because I see things in a different way from them. It's actually a wonderful thing, let's call it our superpower! Tomorrow, we can talk to Miss Fry and see if she can help.'

At school, Miss Fry and Mr Mavjee
made a plan for Trixie.

Slowly, it helped her find new ways of
learning some of the things she found tricky.

The plan

Trixie loved being part of a plan!

In circle time, Miss Fry asked everyone to say what the person sitting next to them was really good at.

Lily said Trixie was the best dancer she'd ever seen.
'We're all good at different things, aren't we?' Trixie said.

'You can run the fastest.'

'You can count the highest.'

Miss Fry smiled.
'You're right, Trixie.'

'You're the kindest.'

'You give the best hugs.'

Trixie decided she didn't mind if she learned things in a different way to her friends. She liked having her own superpower, just like her dad.

Once she stopped worrying so much, she started to have fun dancing with her letters.

letters

leap

school

dance

shimmy

friends

jump

spin

sashay

fun

stories

words   reading

twirl   'Sam has a cat!'

stomp

And soon . . .

. . . Trixie was back to running and jumping and cartwheeling and dancing in Primrose Tower.

So once again everyone could tell when Thunderboots was home!